*For Cesc, Maria and Matilda
and the island of Minorca*

First American edition 1999 by Kane/Miller Book Publishers
Brooklyn, New York & La Jolla, California

Originally published in Great Britain in 1982 by
Blackie and Son Limited, Glasgow and London

Published in Spain in 1982 by Ediciones Hymsa, Barcelona, Spain
under the title (in Catalan) *La Lluna D'en Joan*

Text and illustrations copyright © 1982 by Carme Solé Vendrell

Library of Congress Cataloging-in-Publication Data

Solé Vendrell, Carme, 1944
[Lluna d'en Joan. English]
Jon's moon / Carme Solé Vendrell. — 1st American ed.
p. cm.
Summary: With the moon's help, Jon rescues his fisherman
father's spirit from an octopus at the bottom of the sea.
[1. Fathers and sons—Fiction. 2. Sea stories. 3. Moon—Fiction.] I. Title.
PZ7.S6877Jo 1999   [E]—dc21   98-36177

Printed and bound in Singapore by Tien Wah Press Pte. Ltd.
1 2 3 4 5 6 7 8 9 10
ISBN 0-916291-87-1

Jon's Moon

By Carme Solé Vendrell

A CRANKY NELL BOOK

Kane/Miller Book Publishers

Brooklyn, New York & La Jolla, California

Close by the sea Jon and his father lived happily together in a solid little cottage which clung to the cliffs.

Every night Jon's father went out to sea to fish.

Every night Jon stayed safely at home with the moon to keep him company.

Then one night there was a terrible storm . . .

The dark, angry sea reared up over the tiny
fishing boat. One huge wave struck Jon's father
such a blow that it drove his spirit out of him.
The precious spirit slipped slowly and silently
to the bottom of the sea.

 With the first light of day Jon's father returned
home. His cheeks were strangely colorless.
His boat was heavy as he dragged
it onto the sand. Painfully he climbed the
steep steps to the house.

That night Jon had not slept at all. The storm had stopped his friend the moon from keeping him company. He had been alone except for the wind, and the wind's howling had made him afraid.

As he tucked his cold, shivering father into bed, Jon knew that he had been right to be afraid. All day he watched over his father, who lay silent, cold and still.

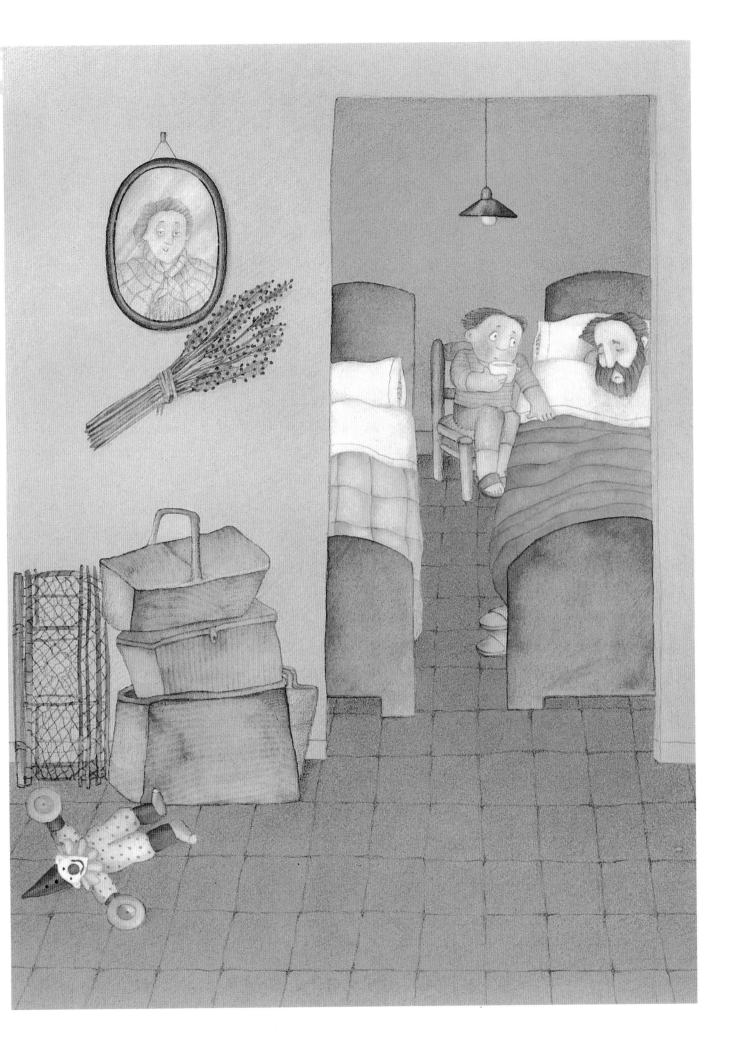

When night came the moon returned, and Jon sobbed out his story to her. The moon promised to help him but told him that he would have to be brave. Together they would search the sea for the spirit of his father.

Jon knew where he had to go. Filled with fear he ran to the cliff-top, to the sailor's cemetery with the lone cypress that reached into the sky. The wind still blew with fury and moaned around the walls of the dark, shadowy cemetery.

The cemetery was full of sighs, but Jon knew that he must run as fast as he could and climb to the top of the tall cypress tree.

As Jon climbed, the moon sank slowly down to meet him. Jon took her gently in his hands and put her in his basket. Now the cemetery was full of light. For a moment Jon paused as he thought of those who rested there.

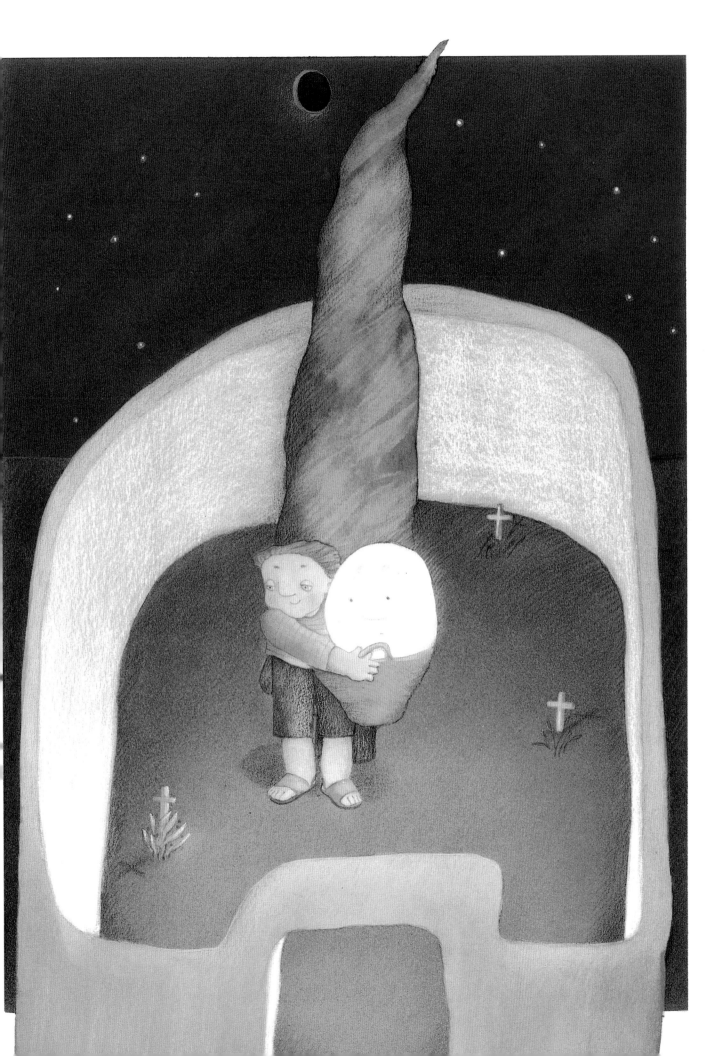

Like a lantern, the moon lit everything in Jon's path. They would have to hurry; the night would be short, and when dawn came they would be too late.

The rocks were like knives and spears that the sea had sharpened all winter long. Rocks that Jon knew so well by day now seemed like menacing giants. The seagulls woke and screamed piercingly at them as they passed, but the moon gave Jon courage.

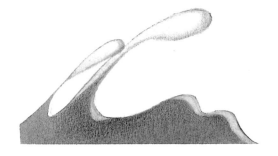

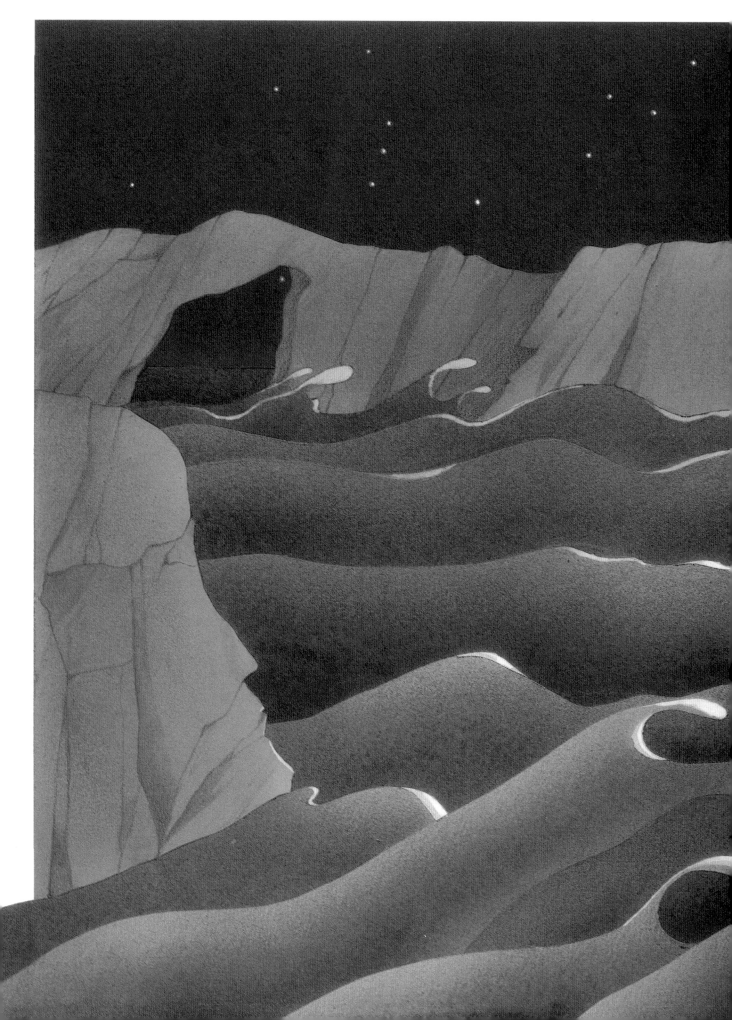

The night began to reflect the approaching dawn. Jon and the moon took a deep breath and plunged into the sea. In a cave far below the waves an octopus had caught Jon's father's spirit and held it in his tentacles.

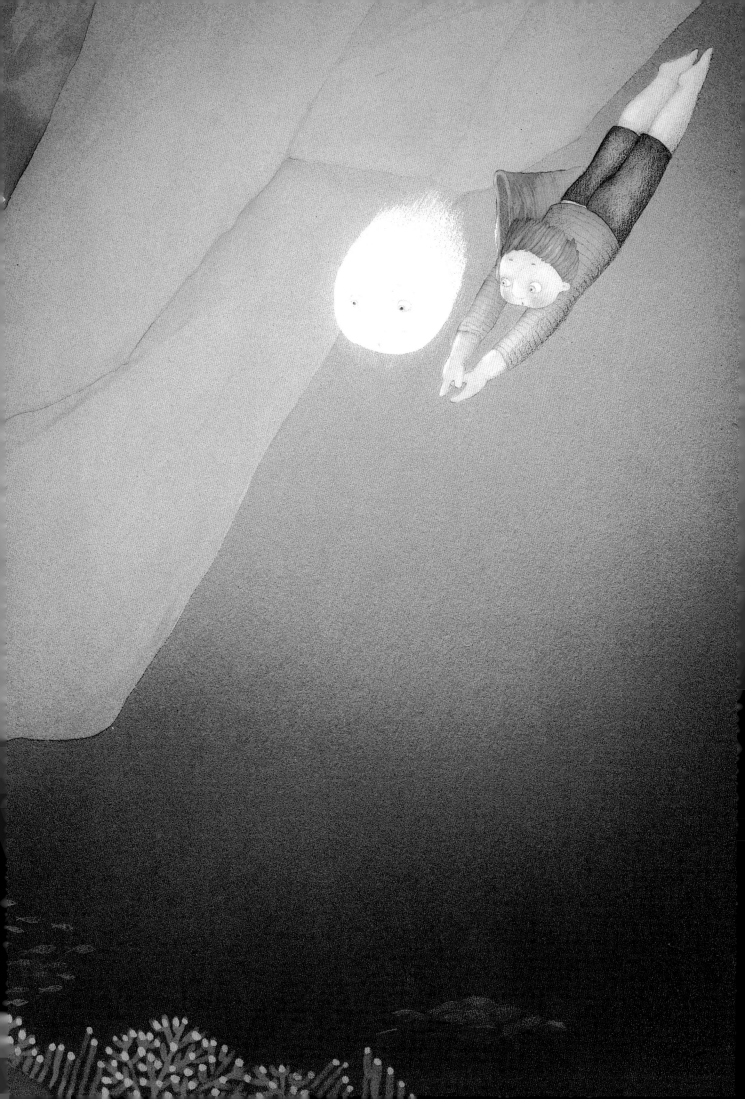

The moon dived downwards, gleaming like a great silver bubble. The octopus was bewitched. Dazzled, he reached out for the moon, forgetting for a moment the precious spirit, which slipped from his grasp. The moon shone with all her brilliance and blinded him. Leaving the octopus helpless, Jon and the moon escaped, taking Jon's father's spirit with them.

carme solé vendrell

The wind was softer now and blew Jon gently home. The sea breathed peacefully, and the moon rose slowly back into the sky.

Jon stretched out his arms
lovingly to his father and restored
his spirit to him. Gradually the
color flooded back into his father's
cheeks.

High in the sky the moon, Jon's moon, smiled.